The

Masquerade

A poetic story celebrating community and love

Tessy Braun

The Midnight Masquerade

ISBN:
9 – 781-7018 -4650 - 0

The Midnight Masquerade

Preface

Thank you for buying "**The Midnight Masquerade**". I really hope that you enjoy reading this poetic story, and that it takes you to a delightfully magical place.

The story was inspired by a word prompt from a magical arts and poetry community on Instagram called **@myth.and.lore** which I have been a part of. I loved the word prompt that I created (*Midnight Masquerade*) and it was from there that this narrative poem was enthusiastically created.

I would very much appreciate if you would like to write an honest review on Amazon and Goodreads.

Love and light

Tessy x

.

The Midnight Masquerade

Contents

The Midnight Masquerade

Acknowledgements

Thank you to all of those who encourage my writing, in particular Billy Harrington (**@thepoetbillyharrington** on Instagram), and my wonderful mother, Rosemary Braun.

The Midnight Masquerade

The Midnight Masquerade

Just before midnight strikes
You'll come across a strange delight,
With bowls of punch and lemonade -
The "***Woodland Midnight Masquerade***"!
The squirrel in his copper suit,
Barn Owl's ready for a hoot,
The Pine Marten fills his glass,
To relish in the razzmatazz!
All await the greeting speech,
Those wise words their leader speaks,
The slinky soul with tufty ears,
Greeted with endless cheering cheers!
The creature who's behind it all,
The one to whom all folk do fall,
The one who sits proud like the sphinx,
The one and only **Woodland Lynx**!

She is adored across the land,
Behind her trail her loyal fans,
In hope to catch a glimpse or gaze,
Her presence leaves them all amazed.
She looks around and twitches her whiskers,
Come from the crowd a wave of whispers -
"I adore her soft sweet paw!"

They clap and clap and cheer on more!
"Her dress is something from the stars!"
"Her sparkling shoes come from a-far!"
"She is a mystic cat of magic art"
"Come Queen - Let this party start!"
She smoothly steps on to the stand,
Her little prince now takes her hand,
"Mama I'm so proud we're here"
The little cub lets out a tear.

It was not very long ago
When dark hunters hurt him so,
And took away his dad the King
Now little prince no longer sings.
He's always very scared at night
That dark hunters may come back to fight
And take him from his forest home,
Leaving mama all alone.
Woodland Lynx raised her head
"It is a very special time" she said.
"It's time to put our past behind,
So a better future we can find.
"We've suffered grief beyond belief
We've prayed our forest be in peace,
We cannot let dark hunters scare,
We cannot let them anywhere!
The scars remain for all to see"
Displaying her leg vehemently.

"These scars are our reminder for
Our loyalty to 'Forest Law'
Tonight I wish you all to eat,
Drink and dance - be on your feet!
We celebrate our fresh new start
Each citizen, you're in my heart!"

From the crowds whistles and gasps,
And tears of sadness for the past,
The awful acts that once took place,
The terror that they had to face.
Yet Woodland Lynx was here tonight
Declaring they had won the fight,
And they were here and not afraid
At the ***Woodland Midnight Masquerade***!

They drink champagne and cheer their host
And raise their glasses in a toast
To celebrate the mystery woods
Eating cakes and chocolate puds!
With speeches done it's time to mingle,
Among the guests a Merry jingle.
And with the call of the fanfaronade
Marked the start of the ***masquerade***!

The little Prince begs his mum
To let him run and have some fun,

But a little fox had looked his way
And called Prince over for a play.
Woodland Lynx kissed her cub
And gave his head a little rub.
"Don't stray too far - keep close by"
She blew a kiss and winked her eye.
The little fox gave Prince a mask
And with a cheeky bark-like laugh,
Said "Let's play a game of hide and seek!
Close your eyes and do not peep!".
Meanwhile the party's in full swing,
The table laid with everything -
Food to spark imagination
Full of choice and pure temptation -
Trifles with sherry custard
Makes the beavers hot and flustered.
Mulled wine with orange spice
Gives giggles to the thirsty mice!
With little bowls of pinewood Jelly,
Jazz rabbits' band give it welly!
A special effort is always made
At the ***Woodland Midnight Masquerade***!
The gents are dressed in velvet coats
Pouring brandy down their throats,
Revelling under starry skies,
Feasting on sloe gin mince pies -
And oh so smart but in disguise

A little mask to hide their eyes,
With feathers poking here and there
And glitter sparkling everywhere!
Smart black shoes and shiny pins
Securing flowers and other things
Like medals or a handkerchief
A ticking clock or maple leaf.
The little stoats in their coats
With satin trim tell party jokes.
They laugh and roll around in jest
In hope that partners they'll impress!

The ladies in their evening best,
Sequins sewn onto each dress
They waltz about light on their toes
Smiling for that perfect pose!
But on their face the mask they made
For this **Midnight masquerade**
Makes it tricky to work out
Who's bill is whose, who owns which snout.
Who's furry arms belongs to who,
To whom each compliment is due?
It adds excitement to the ball
The favourite part for one and all.
By 2 o'clock - no sign of sleep
With woodland folk still on their feet.
Except one that's darting to and fro

Calling "Prince, where did you go!?"
Woodland Lynx weeped and sobbed.
  "Perhaps he's fallen in a bog!"
Then little fox came into mind
And how she was so sweet and kind,
And how she beckoned Prince to play
  Then gently lead her Cub away.
She came to realise through the night
She hadn't checked he was alright.

The potent punch that she had lapped
  Seemed to make the time elapse.
When politely talking with her guests
  She hadn't time to pause for breath!
  And so a team was pulled together
Those of fur and scales and feathers.
  To scour all the forest wide
From the ground and from the sky!

As they searched, Prince stayed hidden
In part of the woods that was forbidden.
He crouched down low with shaking paws
  (He wasn't used to breaking laws).
Prince couldn't hear a single tune,
  Just eerie silence by the moon.
What started off a harmless sport
Had left him in a skunks' resort!
Prince had wandered far and deep,

He opened one eye to take a peep,
He longed to hear the little fox
Cry "Here I am, ready or not!"
"Please will someone find me soon"
Wishing on the stars and moon.
He poked his head up from the space
To determine if his spot was safe.
But in the shadows by the trees,
Were men with rabbits at their knees,
They were dark hunters with their guns,
Belly laughing with their chums.
They heard a rustle in the ferns,
Swung around with eyes that burnt,
Looking for unsuspecting prey
The victim that would come their way.

Prince had frozen in cold fear
To once again be stood so near
To those Dark Hunters of the night
Recalling when he lost the fight.
This had to be a different story!
One that would reflect his glory,
The little lynx thought quickly then
Of how he would defeat these men!
He brought his paw up to his jaw
And felt what he did not know before -
The party mask he'd worn a while
Was a fierce and frightening crocodile!

Now Prince was feeling oh so brave,
The hero of the ***masquerade***!
He made a grunting monstrous squawk
Emerging with a scary walk!

He raised his claws into the air
Opened his jaw and cried "beware!"
A creature with a gator face
With tufty ears looked out of place!
What was this monster of the woods?
A devil here to take their goods?
This loathsome beast has come to feast,
Its teeth are sharp to say the least!

Its scaly nose protrudes so long
And with spotty fur he looks all wrong,
It's something from the depths of hell!
(And has a terribly awful smell!)
Meanwhile the searchers had closed in
And were in witness to the scene,
They watched behind a mossy bank
By now they were quite cold and dank.
They saw the 'monster' rage and roar
Their faith in Forrest Law restored.
Yet Woodland Lynx knew her child
Even with a mask of crocodile!
The hunters screamed and sped away

"These woods are cursed, save us we pray!
Please don't kill us - we are good men,
We'll never hunt these woods again!".

And from behind the bank of moss
Raised twenty faces looking lost,
What a crazy night it's been
None could believe what they had seen!
And Little Prince stood all alone
Thinking of how tonight he'd grown
From a timid cub to feeling brave
At this ***Woodland Midnight Masquerade!***

With a tilted head to Orion's Belt
Prince felt his heart begin to melt.
His little voice let out a scale
(Although it was still somewhat frail).
Then twenty friends emerged to help
A chorus where they all would yelp,
The little Cub then sang once more
Just as he used to once before!
And into mama's arms he flew,
A mother's love so pure and true!
Then he felt a little tap
He quickly looked behind his back.
And just who was there looking pale,
But with big bright eyes and bushy tail?

It was the little fox who led him deep
Into the woods for hide and seek.
"I'm sorry Prince, for what I've done
I was bored and searched for fun.
But you're a hero, you left your mark,
As you defeated hunters dark!"
Then cheers from the joyous crowds rang,
And all the merry folk then sang
Then the band began to serenade
At the ***Woodland midnight Masquerade***!
So all was fine throughout the woods
And all was forgiven and understood.
And danced they did,
And merriment they made
Until the call of the fanfaronade
That marked the end of the ***masquerade***.

About the Author

Tessy has been writing poems and short stories since she was a child. Tucked away in her home you'll find boxes of diaries and journals that are testimony to her love of writing.

In addition to writing, Tessy is also a keen musician and enjoys playing the cello and violin. Tessy is a mother of two young boys and enjoys exploring the outdoors with them.

Tessy would be so grateful if you would like to leave a review of 'The Voice of Six Tudor Queens' on Amazon.

Other titles from the author

For None Would Hear
A poetic story exploring the tragic consequences of domestic abuse.

Open Book
A collection of poetry exploring a range of themes including love, heartbreak, abuse, depression, parenting and loss.

The Midnight Masquerade
An enchanting poetic story celebrating community and love.

Travels with Tessy
A poetic journey throughout South West England and beyond.

In the Little Woodland Clearing
A narrative poem about child-eating faeries and the quest to restore peace in the little woodland clearing.

The Midnight Masquerade

Travels with Tessy

Review

"This is a delightful book which celebrates the often unsung beauty of the English coastlines. I am English but have lived abroad for the last 3 years now and I often get nostalgia for the good old Britishness we should celebrate more. This is why I have especially enjoyed reading this poetry collection this summer as it has helped me feel more connected to my mother country. Tessy Braun takes us on a heartfelt stroll, amble and climb along memory lane as she reflects on the halcyon days of childhood and innocence. Poetically, she makes great use of rhyme which is a joy to read, reflecting the connections between nature and humans. For a lovely summer seaside reading treat, I'd recommend this book to all"

The Midnight Masquerade

For None Would Hear

Review

"*For None Would Hear* is a bold narrative poem filled with atmosphere and imagery. The rhyming scheme is strong and consistent. The piece brings to mind the devastation of Brontë's "Wuthering Heights" and the Gothic haunting landscapes of Walter de la Mere's "The Listeners" and Alfred Noyes' "The Highwayman". A chilling fable of the perils in not seeing the signs before it's too late. The shorter poems included at the end are a welcome addition, with "Each Bird" standing out as a particularly strong allegory for abusive and controlling relationships. Well worth a read!"

Open Book

Reviews

"**Open Book** is an emotional roller coaster. From funny tales, to love, heart break, abuse, and loss. I loved every word and every line! I can't wait to read more of Tessy's work!"

"Fascinating collection of poems guaranteed to move you and inspire you. Tessy has bared her soul in this impressive book".

The Voice of Six Tudor Queens

Reviews

"Six fascinating and historically accurate poems about the wives of Henry VIII. I loved them all, and "Anne Boleyn" was my favourite. Telling the stories from the perspective of each of King Henry's wives is very effective. A great read which includes all of the gory bits!"

"I truly enjoyed reading these beautifully written poems about the 6 wives of King Henry 8th.
I have a keen interest in the Tudors and thought I had read all there was to read about their lives, however Tessy's book has provided more facts I was unaware

of! This has reignited my passion for the Tudors, what an absolute Gem of a book!"

Thank you

Tessy welcomes honest comments on her writing and would be delighted if you would like to leave a review of "The Midnight Masquerade" on Amazon and Goodreads.

Printed in Great Britain
by Amazon